Museum Madness

JoAnn Vergona Krapp
Illustrated by Marianne Savage

This is a work of fiction, but the Royal Museum of Fine Arts and the Museum of Musical Instruments are attractions in Brussels. All references to Bruegel's painting, Landscape with the Fall of Icarus, are well-documented,.and the story of Daedalus and Icarus is a favorite Greek myth.

Publishers Cataloging-in-Publication

Krapp, JoAnn Vergona

Museum Madness by
JoAnn Vergona Krapp

p. cm.

Summary: While visiting Brussels, the Burton family spend an afternoon at the Royal Museum of Fine Arts, where twins Jamie and Lynne inadvertently witness what turns out to be the theft of a famous painting. The twins become an integral part in solving the art theft, but not before their lives are put in danger..

ISBN: 978-0-9722576-7-1
1.   Museums—Juvenile fiction.
2.   Art thefts—Juvenile fiction.
3.   Brussels (Belgium)--Juvenile fiction. I. Savage,
     Marianne, Illus.

II. Title
Fic
Published by
JVKArts
Long Island, New York

DEDICATION
to
MUSEUMS
in appreciation for
endless hours of enjoyment

To Lila,

There's an adventure waiting for you

Also Illustrated by

MARIANNE SAVAGE

ANNIE TILLERY MYSTERY SERIES:
The Madonna Ghost
Girl With Pencil Drawing
The Secrets in the Fairy Chimneys
The Mystery of the Lost Avenger

BUBBLE TROUBLE

SONGBIRD'S FRIENDSHIP SCALE

WHALE ISLAND

THE BUCCANEERS
OF ST. FREDERICK ISLAND

BEYOND A GLUTEN FREE DREAM

J. Ann V. Kruip
4/20/23

Museum Madness

Table Of Contents

Chapter One
The Hotel

Jamie sat at the edge of the hotel bed, arms folded across his chest, lips clenched and teeth gritted, trying to squelch the angry words he was holding back.

But it didn't work.

The words spilled out.

"I still can't believe you're taking us on this vacation. A river cruise! Some vacation. My friend Jeremy went on one last year and said there's nothing for kids to do… no game rooms, no pools, just a lot of old people, sitting in lounge chairs and staring at the water."

Wasn't anyone listening?

"We wanted to try something different," his mother said, shaking the wrinkles from the skirt she took from her suitcase.

"It's different, all right," grumbled Jamie, "if you call 'boredom' different."

Satisfied that the television worked, Mr. Burton stopped fiddling with the tv dials, turned off the set, and faced his son.

"I've had a stressful year at work and I want a relaxing no-brainer vacation."

"But…"

"Oh, stop complaining," his sister Lynne said. "You've been at it since we landed at the airport."

"Oh yeah! The airport. Can you blame me? The Brussels airport was a disaster! We were crowded together, hundreds of wall-to-wall people lugging suitcases, no air-conditioning. It was smelly and sweaty. It was 3 hours before we finally reached the passport agent. And then … then … it took him all of a minute to flip a page and stamp it."

"That's enough, you two," Mrs. Burton declared. "We're tired from the overnight flight. It's only 11 am, so let's lie down for a while. Then we can go to the lobby, have some lunch and talk about stuff to do for the next two days before we meet the cruise ship."

"You heard your mother," said Mr. Burton as he flopped onto one of the double beds.

"Take off your shoes, Jamie. You're bunking with me."

"Great," thought Jamie…" thrilling to have my Dad as a bedmate."

Jamie lay down and let his mind wander. *I could be at camp with my friends. This summer we're eligible for archery and golf. But, no, I'll be stuck on a cruise with the geriatric set.* He imagined different scenarios to keep the family from boarding that ship. Get sick? Get lost? Get caught shoplifting from the hotel gift shop … nah, that would really stretch his dad's patience. *Whatever! I'm going to find a way to miss that boat!*

Chapter Two
The Plan

Jamie felt a gentle touch on his shoulder.

"Wake up, son. You must have had some dream, smiling in your sleep."

Jamie sat up. What was that last thing he remembered? Oh, yeah...his parents frantically yelling to the captain as the last of the passengers boarded the ship. "We can't find our son!"

At least my dreams aren't boring, he thought as they took the elevator down to the lobby.

After lunch, Mrs. Burton spread out a number of brochures highlighting Brussels' attractions. One thing was certain—Brussels had museums, lots of museums, at least twenty, each with a different specialty.

Jamie and Lynne tossed aside the Natural History Museum, the Science Museum and the Military Museum.

"Look at this one," said Lynne, pointing to the Costume Museum. Illustrations of popular fashions from the 1920's decorated the cover.

"What about this?" Jamie picked up the Comic Book Center brochure, with Superheros and villains in serious combat.

"Find one you can agree on," said Mrs. Burton, "or we'll be spending the next two days in the lobby."

Mrs. Burton looked at her two children, fraternal twins, born twelve years ago. *You would never know they were related*, she thought. *Their physical features, their interests, all different. Not a bad thing,* she mused. *They are each their own person.*

"Here's one," suggested Mr. Burton, holding up the brochure for the Museum of Musical Instruments. "Jamie, you play saxophone, and Lynne, you sing in the Junior Chorus."

One look at their father and both know he had made the

decision for them.

"Fine," said Lynne. "What about you guys? Any place you like?"

"Oh, we knew where we wanted to go while you were both sleeping," said Mrs. Burton. "The Royal Museum of Fine Arts."

"An art museum! We live in New York City. You're an art teacher and you practically live at the Met Museum.," said Jamie.

"Yes, but this museum has a famous painting I've always wanted to see and it's rarely on exhibit anywhere." She unfolded the pamphlet and pointed to a photograph with the caption, "Landscape with the Fall of Icarus," by Peter Bruegel.

"Isn't that the guy who built wings that melted when he got too close to the sun?" asked Lynne.

"It's a great story… a Greek myth. I'll tell you about it later," said Mrs. Burton.

The twins laughed. "It's been a long time since you told us a bedtime story."

Chapter Three
The Myth

"Okay, I'm ready." Jamie was curled up under the covers, blanket up to his chin.

"Ready for what?" asked his dad.

"The story, the story about the kid with the wings, you know, the one in the painting," answered Jamie.

Mrs. Burton laughed, putting aside the magazine she was reading. "I'm surprised you haven't studied Greece this year. It's one of their most famous myths.

"It's about an artist and inventor named Daedalus and his young son Icarus. Minos, the King of Crete, wanted to build a home underneath the palace for his pet. Now this was no ordinary pet. It was a Minotaur, a hideous monster with the head of a bull and the body of a human."

"I've seen pictures of a Minotaur," said Lynne. " Ugly, ugly creature. Very strong with glowing red eyes and killer hooves with stabbing nails. It ate human flesh." She smiled at Jamie. "Enough to give you nightmares."

"You're not scaring me. So, what about this Minotaur?" Jamie asked.

"Minos invited Daedalus to come to the palace and build a maze, called a Labyrinth, where the Minotaur could live but never escape," continued Mrs. Burton. "And he did; Daedalus' Labyrinth was so complicated that that the only way out was to be rescued. Minos was delighted and offered Daedalus and Icarus all the comforts of his kingdom."

"Sounds perfect to me," sighed Jamie. "A beautiful island, free food and drink."

"It was perfect," agreed Mrs. Burton, … "but"… she held up a finger … "always a but … until a ship from Athens arrived, carrying several children."

"Were they orphans?" asked Jamie.

"Oh, no!" she answered. "They weren't orphans or

visitors. They were sort-of a payment promised by Athens years ago when Crete attacked Athens. If Crete would leave without attacking, the Athenians would pay a yearly tribute of seven boys and seven girls to feed the Minotaur."

"That's...that's ghoulish! Did they really do that... sacrifice kids?"

"Yes, but this time, there was an Athenian warrior called Theseus with the children. He volunteered to be one of the victims. Theseus was young and handsome. Minos' daughter Ariadne took one look and fell madly in love with him. And ... lucky for him, she persuaded Theseus that, if she helped him kill the beast, he would take her back with him."

"How could he get out of the Labyrinth?" asked Lynne.

"Ariadne took care of that. She gave Theseus two things: a sword that he hid under his tunic and a spool of thread. When he entered the Labyrinth, Theseus unwound the thread and left a trail until he found the Minotaur.

Lucky for him, the creature was asleep. He killed the

Minotaur and followed the thread out of the maze. Before

any of the guards found out, Theseus boarded his boat with

Ariadne and the children and headed back to Athens,

leaving behind the dead Minotaur."

"Minos must've been furious," said Jamie.

"You bet he was," nodded Mrs. Burton. It wasn't long

before he found out, but, by then, Theseus, Ariadne, and the

Athenians, were gone. He blamed Daedalus, the only

person he believed could help anyone escape the maze."

"Did he feed him to the Minotaur?" chuckled Jamie.

Ignoring her son, Mrs. Burton added. "He sent his

soldiers to capture Daedalus and Icarus and imprisoned

them in a tower in Crete.

"Daedalus tried and tried to think of a way to escape

the tower. Every day he watched the birds fly by his

window.

12

"Wings! Why not make wings? He gathered all the bird feathers he could find and glued them together with wax.

"When he had finished two pairs of wings, Daedalus fastened them onto his and Icarus' arms. Before they left,

the father warned his son not to fly too close to the sun or the wax would melt. They flew from the tower and left Crete.

"Young Icarus was thrilled to be flying. He soared higher and higher, forgetting his father's warning. Daedalus was too far to call out to his son. Slowly the sun melted the wings until Icarus fell to earth, plunging into the sea and drowning."

"What happened to Daedalus?" asked Lynne.

"He flew on alone until he reached the island of Sicily, where he lived safely under the protection of the king."

"So that's the subject of this painting you want to see?" asked Jamie.

Mr. Burton took out his laptop and brought up a photo of *Landscape with the Fall of Icarus*.

"All I see is a farmer and some sheep in a field," said Jamie. "So, where's the kid?"

Mrs. Burton pointed to the lower right-hand corner of

14

the painting.

"There…see the legs."

"Weird!" Jamie shook his head. "He fell in head first. Why didn't the artist paint more of the fall?"

"That's another story for another day," said his mother. "Tomorrow you can see the painting and draw your own conclusions."

Chapter Four

The Museum

Chocolate! If one remembered a single sidewalk sight enroute to the museum, it was chocolate. Shop windows displayed tantalizing artistic arrangements of Belgium chocolates in all sizes and shapes.

"We can't just walk past these," groaned Jamie, pointing to a shelf of huge eclairs, chocolate cream oozing from their shells, their tops drizzled with snow white icing.

"On the way back," his mother said, "or they'll melt in your hand instead of your mouth."

The short walk from their hotel took them into Grand Place, Brussels 'crowded city center, checking out the restaurants, the boutiques, the flower market, and the impressive architecture.

An arrow pointed to a hilly area, Mont de Artes, resting between Grand Place and the Royal Museum of

Fine Arts. This was Brussels' cultural hub, lined with art galleries and museums.

"Here it is," said Mrs. Burton. They stood in front of an imposing structure, built centuries ago. It housed three separate museums, with ten floors, containing one of the finest World Art Collections.

"How about that?" Mr. Burton looked at the admission signs. "We get in free today." At that moment the clock on Mont de Artes chimed once. "It's one o'clock and it's the first Wednesday of the month," he smiled. "A freebie."

"Good." said Jamie. "All the more money for chocolate."

"Much too much for anyone to see in one day." Mrs. Burton glanced at the museum map. "The painting I want to see is in the Musee des Beaux Artes. Let's go there first, and, if there's time before closing, we can wander around."

"What about the Music Museum?" asked Lynne.

"Tomorrow," answered Mrs. Burton." We have another day before the boat leaves."

"Oh yeah, the Old Age Boat." Jamie sighed. "At lease I'll have the memory of music and the taste of chocolate".

"You can always make yourself useful, like pushing their wheelchairs and polishing their canes," laughed Lynne.

"Very funny! And what are you going to do for the week?"

"I'm a lot friendlier than you. Besides, it'll be like taking a vacation with Grandma and Grandpa, lots of Grandmas and Grandpas."

"Well, you can be Little Mary Sunshine. I'll be charging my phone to whip up some action games." said Jamie. "It's better than total boredom."

Chapter Five
The Painting and the Poem

An elevator ride took the Burtons to the Musee of Beaux Arts, where a visitor can see one of the largest collections of Dutch painters.

"There." Mrs. Burton pointed." She led them over to a large oil painting that dominated other surrounding paintings by its sheer size, almost two feet by four feet.

A security guard stood near the painting. "Stand behind the white line and no flash photos," he announced.

"So, tell me again why you want to see this?" Jamie asked his mother.

"It's the subject of a poem that I teach in my Art classes."

"Down In the corner," said Mr. Burton, "there -- you can see the legs of Icarus. It's easy to miss. A quiet landscape: a farmer plowing his field, a shepherd tending his sheep, a ship on a peaceful sea." He paused. "And no one notices a drowning person."

"Or, no one cares," said Lynne. "That's so, so ..." She searched for a word.

"Disturbing." whispered Mrs. Burton. "That's what the poem is about.

"This painting is actually a copy. The original was painted by Peter Breugel the Elder in the mid 1500's. His had Daedalus in it. But the original was lost and his son painted the copy, almost exactly the same, but no Daedalus. No one knows why."

"Is this what I have to look forward to in high school?" smirked Jamie.

"Only if you're in my class."

"Take your notes," said Mr. Burton. "We'll wander around the floor. Stay close, you two."

Laptop in hand, Mrs. Burton found a seat opposite the painting and began her study of Landscape with the Fall of

Icarus.

Mr. Burton was happy to check out other Dutch paintings. The twins sauntered around, looked at a few paintings, then headed to the back wall where they could people-watch.

"Hey, Jamie. Look at that guy, the one with the hat. He keeps walking back and forth in front of that Icarus painting."

"He's probably a teacher like Mom. See, he has a clipboard, probably taking notes."

"I don't think so. He's not even looking at the painting, just walking back and forth. You know, like, when someone looks at a painting and moves on to see the next one." Lynne took out her phone and snapped a photo of the man. At the same time, the man dropped his clipboard so that it banged to the floor in front of the security guard. As the guard bent down to pick up the clipboard, the man quickly leaned toward the painting and placed something under the

frame. His action was so swift that it was done before the
guard straightened up.

"Be more careful, sir," the guard said as he handed the
clipboard to the man.

"Sorry about that. Thanks," nodded the man.

Lynne snapped another photo, the man and the guard facing each other.

"That was strange," said Lynne." Everyone knows you can't touch the paintings in a museum. I'm surprised there was no buzzer or something."

"Well, that's why there are guards in every room."

The man moved on, but not before he glanced around the room, his eyes focusing on the back wall.

Lynne noticed the guard looking in the same direction.

She slipped her phone out-of-sight and turned back towards the wall.

"What's with you?" asked Jamie. "You're acting weird."

"Just a funny feeling I had when that guy looked back here."

Chapter Six
The Art of Chocolate

"Let's go, Lynne, Dad is waving us over to Mom and the painting."

The security guard whispered something to Mrs. Burton as she gathered her notes and laptop and stood up from the bench. As the twins approached their mother, the guard nodded a friendly goodbye. Lynne remained a few steps behind her bother, avoiding eye contact with the guard.

"What was that guard whispering about?" asked Jamie.

He apologized for the loud noise the clipboard made, hoped it didn't disturb my studying, "she answered.

"Did you see who dropped it?" asked Lynne.

"I heard the bang but didn't bother to look up." Mrs. Burton paused and looked around. "How about we take our time leaving so I can look at a few more Dutch paintings? I doubt our Met will ever have such an exhibit."

Jamie groaned. "Chocolate...please, before the shops close."

"Relax," said Mr. Burton. "You'll get your chocolate."

Mrs. Burton was mesmerized by the sight of so many Dutch paintings as they walked slowly through several rooms.

They exited through the gift shop and onto the street.

If Dutch art was Mrs. Burton's fantasy, the chocolate shops were Jamie's. Brussels is the chocolate capital of Belgium. From one tantalizing shop to the next, Jamie's taste buds almost exploded. He passed pralines, cakes, bonbons, waffles, truffles, and concoctions whose names he couldn't even pronounce. He marveled at one shop that crafted chocolate tools that fit inside a handyman's kit, made of chocolate, of course. What did he settle on? A confectionary masterpiece: chocolate whipped cream, layered between bittersweet chocolate cake, topped with a fudgy chocolate glaze, and perfected with multi-colored sprinkles. One bite … Jamie closed his eyes and murmured "aah, heavenly, simply heavenly." The rest of the family opted for coffee mousse and hazelnut chocolate bars.

"Wait, Before we leave, I want a photo of Jamie with that creamy stuff oozing all over his mouth.

He's got clown lips," laughed Lynne. Jamie posed as his sister pulled her phone from a back pocket.

"Hey!" she yelled.

"What?" asked Mrs. Burton.

"Someone just tried to grab my phone!"

"Did you see anyone?" asked her dad.

"No. It happened so fast. Somebody bumped into me and all I saw was a hand reaching into my pocket."

"Keep your phone inside your bag," said Mrs. Burton. "Wherever there are crowds, there are bound to be pickpockets."

Back at the hotel, the Burtons made plans for their last day in Brussels, a visit to the Museum of Musical Instruments.

"Let's see that photo you took of me," said Jamie.

"Mousse Mouth. Maybe I should enlarge it for the

class yearbook."

As she put her phone away, Lynne had a sudden flashback to the art museum … the visitor and the guard.

"You look weird again," noticed Jamie. "Now what?"

"Remember the pictures I took of that guy with the hat and the guard? Why did they look back at us?"

"You watch too many spy movies. Forget it. The best part of today was the chocolate. And tomorrow, let there be music."

Chapter Seven
The Sound of Music

As the Burtons walked the short distance from their hotel to the Museum of Musical Instruments, Mr. Burton glanced at the brochure he had taken from the hotel lobby.

"How about this, Jamie? Your saxophone was invented by Adolphe Sax, right here in Belgium."

"You think we'll get to play any of them?" asked Jamie.

"Probably not. We'll see when we get there."

Compared to the brightly lit Museum of Fine Arts, this one had soft lighting that invited a feeling of calm. And, despite the number of people milling around, it was surprisingly quiet. They picked up headphones and portable audio players.

"Do we really need these headphones?" asked Jamie.

"If you want to understand what you're looking at,"

answered Mr. Burton. "The signs are written in French and Dutch, but the audio is programmed for English."

"Can we wander and meet up with you?" asked Lynne.

"All right. It's noon, so let's meet at the gift shop at two," said Mrs. Burton. "I'd like to pick up something small to take home. But you two, stay together." she insisted.

"And don't be late," she added. "We have to repack tonight and arrange to be at the dock tomorrow morning at nine." She looked directly at her son. "Understand?"

"Yes, maam," Jamie saluted. "Musn't keep the old folks waiting."

Mrs. Burton shrugged, something she'd been doing a lot lately.

They split up, adjusted their headphones, and were off.

Jamie and Lynne looked at the directory and decided to start in the basement where the mechanical instruments were housed, and work their way upstairs to the stringed instruments and keyboards.

They strolled from floor to floor, saw and listened to dozens of musical instruments, marveling at their sizes and shapes.

Lynne checked the time. "I can't believe we've been walking around here for two hours. We better get to the gift shop."

The elevator door stopped and Jamie and Lynne stepped out, looking for their mother.

"There she is," Jamie pointed. "She's at the cash register. Looks like she's talking to some guy."

A few steps forward and Lynne stopped dead. "That's not 'some guy.' That's the guard from the museum, the one whose picture I took."

"How do you know that?" asked Jamie. "You have radar or something?"

"Because that weird feeling just came back. I'm getting back into the elevator."

"Too late," said Jamie. "Mom saw us and she's calling us over." His sister's face, froze, as if she'd seen a ghost.

Walking behind her brother, Lynne side-stepped the man to avoid facing him. "Shouldn't we be going now,

Mom?"

"Not yet. I was just about to buy this tiny mechanical piano to take home when who should be at the same place. Remember the guard at the museum, near the painting I was studying. You know, the one who picked up the man's clipboard. Here he is. Some coincidence, huh?"\J

Coincidence? Lynne knew this was no coincidence.

The guard greeted the twins with a broad smile. "Looks like your family chose to visit two of the best museums in Brussels. Kind of overwhelming, isn't it? Hundreds of instruments from around the world. Did you have a favorite?"

When neither one answered, he said. "My favorite is the bagpipe. Your mom told me you're going on a river cruise tomorrow. Too bad your visit is so short. I hoped you had no trouble booking a hotel in this part of town."

"Oh, no. We checked right into The Hyatt, just walking distance to the museums," answered Mrs. Burton.

"Did you have time to visit the shops?" The guard smiled. "Especially the chocolate shops. You know, Belgium does have the best chocolate."

"We should be getting back," said Mr. Burton. "I have to call the cruise director to double check the times."

"Before you go, let me take a photo of the four of you," said the guard.

"Wonderful," agreed Mrs. Burton. "Lynne, use your phone. My battery's gone dead."

Lynne clutched her bag to her chest. "I think I left it in the hotel."

"Nonsense," remarked her mother. "You and that phone are attached. Look in your bag."

Lynne pretended to rifle through her bag. "Nope, it's not here."

"With all the junk you carry around, it's probably down at the bottom. Let me take a look."

"Never mind," said Lynne, pretending to search the

bag again. "Here, I have it." She pulled out the phone and held it tightly.

The guard waited.

Lynne handed him the phone.

The Burtons posed for the photo.

Lynne waited … and watched.

"I'll take another for good measure," he said.

He snapped the second photo.

Lynne wondered, *Why is he taking so long to give me back my phone?*

"I'm sure you'll have some lovely pictures of Brussels, even in the short time you were here. Enjoy the rest of your vacation. It was a pleasure to meet you."

As the guard left for the elevator, Jamie shook his head. "Geez, Mom. You told all that to a stranger in a strange town. I hope you didn't give him your social security number too."

The Burtons took the elevator to the ground floor.

Lynne whispered to her brother. "Did you see how long he held my phone? I betcha anything he wanted to scroll through my pictures."

"Yeah, it was kind of creepy that he showed up here," agreed Jamie.

Outside the museum, Mr. Burton spied a newspaper kiosk. "Let me pick up a paper ... see what's happening in this part of the world."

Chapter Eight
The Missing Painting

Mr. Burton took his newspaper and eased himself into the leather chair, relishing the quiet of their hotel room. After a day of sightseeing, dinner, and repacking, he felt he deserved these few minutes of peace. Mrs. Burton and the twins had opted for an early bedtime.

Mr. Burton jumped up. He rushed over to his wife and gently shook her shoulders, whispering, "Doris, wake up."

"Mmmm, is it morning already?" she mumbled.

"No, no. Just wake up. You have to see this."

A groggy Mrs. Burton reached across the nightstand for her glasses. "What are you waving at me?"

"Read this!" He pointed to the newspaper's headlines:

ART THEFT: FAMOUS BRUEGEL STOLEN

Mrs. Burton slipped out of bed and switched on a lamp. Together they read:

Peter Bruegel's famous 'Landscape with the Fall of Icarus' was stolen after a daring break-in at the Royal Museum of Fine Arts. Part of the Museum's permanent collection, Bruegel's work was the only painting taken. Brussels police believe that the break-in involved someone familiar with the alarm system. According to the museum director, the alarm is checked each night at closing. When the doors opened yesterday morning, the alarm system had been turned off. Police further speculate that the painting was specifically targeted to be sold to a private art collector.

"I sat right in front of it for at least a half hour," said Mrs. Burton. "How creepy is that?"

"What's creepy?" Lynne said, rubbing her eyes.

"That painting I was studying. It was stolen last night," said Mrs. Burton. "Funny thing is it was the only one taken."

Lynne scrambled out of bed.

"Let me see that paper." Her eyes flew over the article.

"I knew it! I knew it!" she cried out.

"What are you yelling about?" Jamie sat up. He saw them hunched over the newspaper. "What're you reading?"

"Look at this." Lynne snatched the newspaper from her father and pointed to the headline. "See …**ART THEFT!** Didn't I tell you something was weird at that museum. That man with the hat and the clipboard, walking back and forth in front of the painting, dropping the clipboard. And that guard. Here, look!"

She reached for her phone and scrolled down to the photos she had taken the day before.

"See, there's the guy and the guard together … and the distraction of the clipboard … and both of them looking back at us when I snapped the photo."

Mr. Burton shook his head. "Your imagination is running wild."

"No, it's not," she insisted, talking louder and faster.

"It makes sense. Remember, after I took the photos, someone tried to grab my phone. And that guard—he must've been following us. Why else would he just **happen** to meet us at the Music Museum?"

Lynne stared at her brother. "Didn't I tell you it was weird?"

"It does make sense," he said. "It's dark in the museum after closing, and there are hundreds of paintings. If only one was stolen, how did the thief know which one to take?"

Mr. and Mrs. Burton reread the article, trying to digest everything the twins had said.

"Give me your phone, Lynne," said Mr. Burton. "I want to see those photos again."

Chapter Nine
The Surprise Attack

After a restless night, Mr. and Mrs. Burton had a decision to make:

"Do we go ahead with our plans and board the boat at noon or do we settle Lynne's suspicions that she has photos that could be important to the museum theft?"

"How can you enjoy a vacation knowing you could help solve a crime?" Lynne blurted out.

"Doris?" Mr. Burton asked.

"She's right. How about we leave our bags in the lobby, find the nearest police station and show them the film. If they think it's helpful, they keep the film and we get a taxi to the pier."

"But I took lots of great photos. And I'm not giving them my phone," insisted Lynne.

"You can't have it both ways, Lynne," declared Mr.

Burton. "Either you think the photos are worth it … or not. We're not forfeiting our vacation because of your imagination."

"C'mon, Lynne," agreed Jamie. "And think about it. The police get your photos and you get a new phone." *And maybe we get to miss the boat after all,* he smiled to himself.

"Well, I want the update!"

Their bags in the lobby, the Burtons left the hotel for the short walk to the police station.

They hadn't gone far when the doors of a black sedan, parked with the motor running, tore open.

Two men jumped out and headed straight for Lynne, walking beside her brother.

"Hey!" yelled Jamie as one of the men grabbed Lynne.

"Let go," she cried out. As Jamie tried to pull him back, the other man grabbed him.

The Burtons, a few yards ahead, turned around and,

hearing their screams, raced toward them. Before

they could reach them, they saw Lynne and Jamie pushed

into the back seat of the car.

Mr. and Mrs. Burton shouted and pounded on the car window as it took off down the road.

Passerbys heard the noise and saw two adults running down the street after a black car.

"That car!" Mrs. Burton pointed to the vehicle as it disappeared into traffic. "They grabbed my kids," she cried out.

"I saw what happened," a man said. "My car's parked right there; let me drive you to the police station."

"I should've listened to her," said Mr. Burton, shaking his head. "They must've been waiting for us."

"Maybe all they want is her phone. It's got the photos from the art museum." Mrs. Burton fought back her tears. "Then they'll let them go."

"No! No!" Mr. Burton cried out. "Lynne doesn't have her phone. Remember, I took it from her last night."

Chapter Ten
The Police Station

Mrs. Burton raced through the doors of the police station.

"Please help us! Our children were kidnapped!"

Mr. Burton and the witness followed right behind her.

"Calm down, Ma'am. I'm Officer Peeters." He pulled out a chair. "Suppose you tell me what's happened."

As she struggled to catch her breath, Mr. Burton began explaining. "It happened so fast. It was unreal, like a movie. There were these two men ..."

It took a while before the police were able to piece together the events leading up to the kidnapping: the museum, the stolen painting, the camera, the guard, the newspaper headline ..."

"Sound to us it's the camera they want. As soon as they have it, they'll let your kids go," the officer reassured them.

"But they **don't** have it." Mr. Burton cried out. "I took my daughter's phone last night." He pulled the phone from his carryon bag. "This is the one they want." He handed it to the officer.

"Let's see what's so important about these photos." He scrolled through pictures until he reached the last few.

"There! Right there," Mrs. Burton looked on. "I was sitting right in front of that painting. I spoke to the guard. Yes, that's the guard. I'd recognize him anywhere. And that's the man who dropped the clipboard. I didn't get a good look at his face but I can describe him better than this photo."

"This was carefully planned." said the officer. "The guard got himself hired to be the plant. The clipboard guy was the distraction to mark the spot targeting that particular painting. When the museum closed at five, the guard shut off the alarm for that wing. Then both guys came back at night; the guard knew exactly where to find the painting.

"Over the years, several famous paintings were stolen this way. Unfortunately, you and your family got in the way. "

"But why steal one painting?" asked Mrs. Burton.

"An art collector!" explained the officer. "A rich citizen wants to add to his private collection. He hires whomever he needs to get inside a museum, like a guard, to target a painting that's priceless, and he waits for the right moment. Obviously, this guard was not a new hire, been working there long enough to be trusted. I bet he'd still be on the job if your daughter didn't take his photo."

"So now what do we do?" asked Mr. Burton.

"Well, sir, my guess is that once the art collector finds out that you're the one with the photos, they'll set up a swap—your kids for the phone."

"You mean we just wait? " said Mrs. Burton.

"Yes, ma'am, we just wait ... I'll get us some coffee."

Chapter Eleven

The Long Ride

Lynne and Jamie sat huddled next to each other.

"I guess your pictures were important for sure," whispered Jamie. "Do you recognize either of these two guys from the museum?"

"No, I only got a good look at the guard and he's not one of them."

"Hey, you two back there," a raspy voice called out. "Keep quiet."

Jamie took a deep breath to lower his voice, trying to sound older. "Where are we going?"

"We're not your chauffeurs. Just keep your mouths shut. No questions. You'll know when we get there," answered the driver.

Lynne folded her hands, then unfolded them. She spread her fingers apart, pulling on each finger.

"Cut that out, Lynne," said Jamie.

"I can't help it. Would you rather I crack my knuckles instead?"

"Do I have to gag you two?" shouted the man in the passenger seat.

"You can't expect us to sit back here, not knowing who you are and where we're going! "Jamie shot back.

"Makes no difference to you who we are 'cause you're never gonna see us again," the driver answered. "Now shut up. We'll get there when we get there."

Jamie moved closer to his sister and whispered, "Let's concentrate on where the car is passing so we can tell the police when they let us go."

"You mean, if they let us go."

"They don't want us, Lynne. They want your phone ... the photos from the museum. That's what they want. And they sent these two goons to take us to the person who wants them."

"But Dad took my phone!" Lynne lashed out.

"Yes, but they don't know that. When we get to wherever they're taking us, give them my phone. When they realize there's no museum photos, they'll let us go."

Jamie slipped his phone into her bag. He patted his sister's hand. "Now, let's just see where they're taking us. Look to see if we pass anything unusual."

"Like what? We're in the country now. It's all the same … farms, houses, barns ..."

"Hey, look at that barn," whispered Jamie, pointing to a bright purple barn. "Somebody's an artist. They painted flowers all over the doors."

"Yea, either that or they're color blind," smirked Lynne.

Chapter Twelve
The Mansion

"Look at this place!" whistled a wide-eyed Jamie.

The car pulled into a long driveway with a black wrought iron gate. The driver spoke into a remote. "We're here." After a few seconds, the gate slowly opened and he drove inside.

Jamie and Lynne stared out the window as they passed what seemed like miles of brick and stone patios, perfectly manicured lawns, dozens of silk draped windows, two swimming pools, a tennis court.

They stopped in front of a double door at the back of the house.

The door opened.

"Okay, we're here." The two men got out of the car and opened the back door. "Get out." He yanked the twins out of the car. "In there," the driver pointed to the open door. "Go in, keep quiet, and wait—and don't do nothin' stupid."

As Jamie and Lynne silently stepped inside, they heard the door shut and the car drive away.

They were in a dimly-lit room, bare of furniture other than a wooden bench in one corner and a closed door in the other. Lynne reached for her brother's hand and they wordlessly moved toward the bench.

No one appeared.

They sat down.

There was nothing to do but wait.

Five minutes felt like five hours ... and then the door opened.

An elderly man in a black suit walked over to them.

"I'm Edward. Jamie and Lynne, right. You must be tired and hungry." he smiled. "Follow me."

The twins exchanged glances. *Must be the butler,* they thought.

Whoever he was, he led them into a cavernous room that resembled a Victorian replica. "It's like one of the showroom galleries at our Met," whispered Lynne. Sofas covered in floral silk patterns; velvet armchairs with plush pillows; cabinets, bureaus, bookcases, and tables carved with intricate woodwork; polished wood floors; paintings and portraits on every wall.

"Beautiful, isn't it?" Edward said proudly to the awestruck visitors.

"Who lives here … the King of Belgium?" asked Lynne.

Edward laughed. \|
"No, our King lives in the Royal Palace in Brussels. This is the ancestral home of a gentleman whose family has lived for generations here in Brussels. He is most anxious to meet you. Now, follow me, please."

The twins tried capturing as much of the furnishing and paintings as they moved into another room.

"Not as splendid as the one you just left," said Edward, "but rather comfortable, don't you think?"

Smaller but equally rich and inviting, they were led to a finely-polished table and chairs, where a pitcher of chocolate milk and a plate of biscuits and chocolates were placed.

"Help yourselves," said Edward, "especially the chocolates. You know that Belgium chocolates are world famous. Take your time. The gentleman of the house will be with you shortly."

Lynne wanted to pinch herself. "Is this day for real?"

Jamie thought back to his dream about missing the riverboat. *Maybe this was supposed to happen; maybe I have some kind of esp.*

Their imaginings came to a halt with the entrance of another man.

"Good afternoon, Jamie and Lynne Burton. Welcome to my home. You many call me Leon."

The twins took one look at Leon and snapped to attention as if given an order.

Leon looked like a military officer—tall and erect, clean-shaven, short hair, a meticulous dark blue suit. The only things missing were the medals and ribbons. He reeked of authority.

The tenor of his voice matched his elegant bearing and the splendor of his home – rich, very rich.

"Please sit and enjoy the snack that Edward prepared for you. Then we have business to discuss." He turned towards the door. "I will return shortly."

Before Jamie and Lynne could say a word, he left the room.

"Mom always says that stress makes you hungry. She was right," said Lynne. "I'm into these chocolates."

Jamie shook his head. "How can you eat at a time like this? Who knows what this guy Leon means by 'business?'"

"C'mon. Jamie. Just sit down."

So, there they were: two young people sitting in a strange room, belonging to a strange man, with no idea where they were, wondering what comes next.

Chapter Thirteen
The Familiar Face

Leon did return shortly, as promised. He approached the twins, still sitting at the table. Looking down at the empty plate of biscuits and chocolates, he smiled.

"Well. now that you're rested, we can talk," he said calmly. "I'll start."

"You have something I want," he said, fixating his eyes on Lynne"s pocketbook. "Give me your phone, young lady."

Lynne looked across at her brother.

"Now!" ordered Leon.

Without a word, she reached into her bag and pulled out the phone.

"Hand it to me, please." Leon stepped beside her chair.

Phone in hand, he began scrolling down the photos until the end.

"Where are the museum pictures?"

"I deleted them!" Lynne blurted out before she even realized what she'd said.

Jamie stood up, facing Leon. "She's right. She deleted them in the car."

"Now why would you do that?" accused Leon.

"Well," she thought fast, "I was running out of space so I deleted some to make room for the rest of our vacation."

Leon's face lost all traces of politeness.

"Why do you two think you are here? This is not a social visit. If the photos aren't here, where are they?" he demanded.

"She told you." answered Jamie. "She deleted them."

Leon's face reddened. "We'll see about that."

"Alfred!" he called out.

In walked Alfred.

The twins looked as if they'd seen a ghost"You ...

You're the guard!" exclaimed Lynne. "The guard from the museum … where the painting was stolen."

"Smart young lady. Too smart," sneered Alfred.

Leon passed the phone to Alfred. "Check out these photos. She says she deleted the museum ones."

Alfred went through all the photos on the phone and, when he reached the end, he reversed the last few to double check, then announced, "This isn't her phone. I looked through her camera at the Musical Instruments Museum and nothing on this phone matches what I saw."

Leon took a deep breath and exhaled slowly. "So... where's the one I want?"

He stared at Jamie. "Sit back down. One of you better come up with the right answer or you're going to be my 'guests' for a long time."

As the two men left the room, Alfred looked back at Lynne. "I wouldn't get him any angrier than he is. I've worked for him for years and he's not known for his patience."

Chapter Fourteen

The Long Wait

Mr. and Mrs. Burton sat at the police station in a small interview room where they could discuss the next step to getting back their children.

"By now, the one responsible for the theft and the kidnapping has figured out he doesn't have the pictures he wants," Officer Peeters said. "We can id the guard as being in on the theft. The museum gave us his address and my men are headed over to his home, but, since he didn't show up for work today, he obviously realizes we know who he is and there's no way they'll find him there."

"My son still has his phone. Why can't we call and work out a deal with the kidnapper?" asked Mr. Burton.

"Because any deal is gonna involve giving him your daughter's phone. We can't allow you to do that because we need those photos for evidence," explained the officer.

"You can't use my kids as guinea pigs," declared Mrs. Burton. "We can walk out of here right now, call my son and set up a trade." She stood up.

"M'aam, M'aam, please, sit down. You're right. But this man is a criminal. Don't you want justice for your children?"

"What I want is my children, safe and sound," she demanded.

"Just give us a few hours," he asked. "They'll be in touch with us. They're art thieves, not kidnappers. In the meantime, we'll copy the photos. We can do the trade. We can nab this guy who obviously has been responsible for other stolen museum thefts. You'll be doing our country a tremendous service."

"Doris," Mr. Burton placed his hand on his wife's shoulder. "Think about it. This man, whoever he is, who has our children, didn't plan on kidnapping them. He has his painting and once he gets the photos, he'll let our kids go."

Mrs. Burton calmed herself. "Okay," she nodded to the officer. "But you have to copy those pictures now, because I want to hear my kids' voices and know they're all right."

"We're on it," said the officer. "We'll make contact with them within the hour. Your kids will be back here before you know it. And, knowing kids, they'll have quite a story to tell you."

Chapter Fifteen
The Gallery

"Where're you taking us?" asked Jamie. "And who are all these people." Alfred was leading the twins down several long hallways filled with statues.

"Famous artists and composers," answered Alfred. "Leon appreciates all forms of fine art. You can look but don't touch."

"This reminds me of the summer we visited the Vatican in Italy," remarked Lynne. "Remember how the halls had all those statues. And, look," she pointed to a room they were passing. "There's even a room with maps, like the Vatican."

"Yes," said Alfred. "Leon is a world traveler ... been to all of Europe's capitals."

"Especially the ones with museums, I bet," said Jamie. "Like Madrid and the Prada, Paris and the Louvre. What about New York and the Metropolitan Museum of Art —

been there too?"

"Cut out the wisecracks, kid. You forget that you two are a major inconvenience."

"What about you," asked Lynne. "You go everywhere with him?"

"Usually," answered Alfred. "We work well together."

"And," she added. "I suppose you get paid well."

"Let's just say I have no trouble paying my bills," he smirked.

They stopped in front of a door rimmed with gold insets and two thick locks.

Alfred pulled out a keychain and proceeded to open both locks. He swung open the door. "Go in," he ordered.

Their first thought was, *We're getting locked up in this room.* But fear turned to wonder as they looked around.

"Welcome to Mr. Leon's Gallery." Alfred circled his arms around the room as their eyes scoured the walls. The room was spacious. Wood-paneled walls, windows covered with red velvet draperies, two chandeliers, and a large grand piano.

"What's wrong? Cat got your tongues," laughed Alfred. "Didn't expect this, did you?"

Paintings. Wall–to-wall paintings.

"Leon calls it his 'Magic Garden.' You're looking at some of the world's greatest art."

"Oh, my God." Lynne blurted out. "Did he steal all these?"

Alfred couldn't help smiling. "Of course not. Leon is an extremely wealthy man. Some are original pieces he bought from art galleries. Some weren't for sale so he paid for reproductions."

"You mean forgeries," said Jamie.

"Poor choice of words," scowled Alfred.

"Look, Jamie," Lynne pointed. "There's the Icarus one."

"Yes," said Alfred. "That one, and some of the others," he paused, "were a little harder to acquire."

"I don't understand," said Lynne, 'Why would someone spend so much time and money to get all these paintings and then lock them up where no one can see them?"

"You're wrong, young lady. Someone does see them. Mr. Leon. This is his private museum where he can spend hours admiring the creative genius of world-famous painters and the beauty and peace their works bring to him."

"You're the one who's wrong," snapped Jamie. "Someone else sees them. Me and my sister. And when we get outta here, we'll tell the police where this place is. So Mr. Leon better enjoy it while he can."

Lynne gabbed her brother's arm. "Shut up, Jamie."

Alfred shook his head. "That won't happen. By the time we let you two go, even if you can eventually lead the police here, we'll be long gone."

"He's gonna leave all these paintings?" Lynn couldn't believe it.

"Of course not," Alfred said. "They're going with us."

"That's impossible," exclaimed Jamie "No way you can stuff them into suitcases and hop a plane."

Alfred laughed. "Leon has his own private fleet of planes and he's a pilot himself. As I said, we'll be long gone."

"Yeah," sneered Jamie. "Some place where there's a museum."

Alfred looked at his watch. "Enjoy the view. By now, Leon will have contacted your parents and we'll know what happens next."

Chapter Sixteen
The Plan

"How long does it take to copy a few photos?" Mrs. Burton fiddled with the handles of her pocketbook.

Mr. Burton paced the floor, looking at the notices on the bulletin board.

At that moment, Captain Peeters returned to the room, accompanied by another uniformed officer. "We're done with the photos. Now we wait for the call."

"Why can't we call them now?" asked Mr. Burton. "Jamie has his phone."

Captain Peeters nodded to the officer standing beside him. "This is Detective Janssen. He'll be making the call. He's experienced with hostage situations."

"Hostage situations!" gasped Ms. Burton.

Detective Janssen shot a disapproving look at the Captain. "Sorry for the poor choice of words. Please understand that your children were not part of the plan for the museum theft. We're sure that the person responsible is a wealthy art collector looking to add to his private gallery. Now that his plan has hit a snag, he'll want to cover his identity, perhaps even leave the country. He's just as anxious to get your children back to you as you are. He'll be calling when he has his Plan B ready."

Mr. Burton sat down next to his wife. He placed his hand over hers and whispered, "It'll be all right, Doris; it'll be all right."

At the mansion, Alfred led the twins out of the gallery back to the parlor where Leon was waiting.

"I need time to get the paintings and a few other items out of here. I'll lock up the rest. I've got the planes ready and the vans are on the way to transport everything. I just need to make arrangements with flight control. I'll be piloting one of the planes."

"What do you want me to do?" asked Alfred.

"I was going to have you drive these two back to the

city, get the phone, and drive back here, but that takes too long. I called the two guys who brought them here. They'll take the kids to a public place in the city. I'll call the parents when I know where the kids are and tell them to bring the phone with the photos. That gives us enough time to pack up and leave. You just stay with them for now."

Leon motioned for Jamie and Lynne to sit on one of the sofas. "You two are going home, so don't cause Alfred any trouble. I'm keeping your phone," he said to Jamie. "Try to think of this as an unexpected adventure. And," he smiled, "an excuse to get new phones."\l

Before either of them could speak a word, Leon left.

Jamie poked his sister. "What?" she asked.

"Just follow along," he whispered.

"Alfred, could you get us some water for the car ride, please?" asked Jamie.

Alfred stared at him. "No funny stuff. I'll be right back."

As soon as he left, Jamie hurriedly told his sister they needed to try to find out where Leon was going so the police could find him. "Get him talking, Lynne."

"Why me?"

"Because if I start asking him questions, he'll say I'm being nosy, but you're a girl and he'll be flattered."

Alfred was right back with two bottles of water.

Jamie gave his sister that "do it" look.

"I still can't believe Leon could leave so many wonderful things behind," said Lynne. "It must've taken the family years and years to get all this stuff."

"Oh, there's plenty more," said Alfred. "The family has houses all over Europe. Leon always has a place to call home."

"And you get to travel with him. Lucky you. Do you have a favorite place?"

"Not really. But I must say his home in Madrid is even more splendid than this one. And we haven't been there is a few years."

"And …" Lynne struggled to come up with more questions. "Are you a pilot too?"

"Oh, no. I'm just a passenger. Leon's been flying for years. He has a private airfield where he keeps his planes. In fact, he even has one in Madrid."

It was obvious that Alfred took great pride working for Leon.

Chapter Seventeen

The Swap: Part One

Once again, Jamie and Lynne found themselves in the back seat of the same black car.

"Same rules as before," said the driver. "No talking and no phone. Hand it over."

Jamie reached over to the front seat and handed his phone to the guy in the passenger seat.

"Take a nap, look out the window, whatever," the driver said, "only no nonsense."

The twins were so relieved to be going back to their parents that they simply watched the countryside.

"Can you go a little faster?" asked Jamie, noticing that the driver was well within the posted speed limit.

"Clever, aren't you? I speed and get stopped by the police. No way."

Lynne nudged her brother. "Don't get him mad. We

just wanna get back."

"Fine," said Jamie. "At least let's check out the landmarks. Remember that purple barn. Look for more unusual stuff."

Countryside is pretty much the same: large fields with a house and barn, a pickup truck or tractor, wildflowers, mountains in the distance, stone borders, cattle here and there.

Lynne was envisioning her new phone when Jamie poked her and pointed outside.

Not far from that purple barn was a white house with polka dots painted on the front door. Next to it was a hot pink station wagon. Further down the same field was the tractor, not the usual John Deere kind. This was painted orange and black with the number 34 on it.

"Looks like these country folk added a little color to their lives," smiled Lynne. "Good for them. Except I would've used different colors on the tractor."

That was the highlight, The rest of the trip was unremarkable … more farms, trees, small ponds, more farms.

After a while, the car passed the outskirts of a city. Gas stations, motels, fast food places.

Then the sign—downtown Brussels 2 miles.

Jamie made a mental note.

Soon … activity! A town fair was underway, smack full of people, cars parked in a large grassy field.

"Perfect." the driver pulled into an empty spot and tuned off he engine. Using his remote phone, he dialed the mansion.

Leon answered on the first ring. "Where are you?"

Right outside a Renaissance Fair in Brussels on Route 24. I'm parked next to a yellow bus with license plate EFT 3733." It's 2:50 pm and the place is mobbed with people and booths."

"Fine," said Leon. "Keep the kids in the car. I'll call

the parents now. The boy gave me his father's mobile number. I'll call you back as soon as I arrange for the swap."

"Swap?" asked the driver.

"The phone for the kids. Now remember what you have to do."

Chapter Eighteen

The Swap: Part Two

Mr. Burton's mobile rang. Mrs. Burton jumped up and yelled for Officer Peeters.

The officer placed a pad and pencil next to the phone. "Repeat everything he tells you." he whispered to Mr. Burton.

"Who is this?" answered Mr. Burton, trying to keep a calm voice.

"You know why I'm calling," said the voice at the other end of the phone. "Your children are fine and are in Brussels waiting for you. Listen carefully and follow my directions."

"Yes, yes." said Mr. Burton. "Just speak slowly so I get it right."

"You and Mrs. Burton will drive alone—no police— just the two of you—to the Renaissance Fair in Brussels on

87

Route 24. Bring the girl's phone. When you reach the fairgrounds, there is a large grassy parking area. Do not park there or the driver will leave with your children. I repeat: DO NOT PARK THERE. Find a place on the street where you can walk into the area. I will call you back in a few minutes and tell you where to meet your children."

Leon hung up and called the driver. "Look around the area and find a food booth where the kids can meet their parents. I don't want them to see you or your car."

The driver stepped out and walked a few yards to the perimeter of the parking area. From there he saw a food booth with a bright yellow and green awning. He called Leon.

"Okay. I'm calling the parents to set up the meeting."

Leon gave Mr. Burton the final instructions: " Walk through the fair and wait in front of a food booth with a bright yellow and green awning. Remember to come alone and bring the phone."

Officer Peeters hurried the Burtons into an unmarked police car. "The fair is about fifteen minutes from here. When you get there, I'll drop you off. Get to the food booth and wait. The driver will be watching you from wherever he's parked. Once he sees you meet your children, he'll drive away."

Jamie and Lynne sat very still in the car.

"What are we waiting for?" asked Lynne.

"He's setting up a swap," answered her brother.

"Whatever. All I know is I'm tired and hungry."

The driver returned to the car just in time to hear Lynne's last few words …"I'm hungry."

"Good news. You're meeting at a food booth."

"Sometimes I think your stomach has a direct line to your brain, "quipped Jamie.

The driver checked his watch. "In ten minutes, you come with me," he told Jamie. "We'll watch from the edge of the lot. Your sister stays in the car with my friend. She can sit there and decide what she wants to eat."

The Burtons arrived at the food booth as planned.

"Are you sure they can see us?" asked Mrs. Burton.

"Maybe I should've worn something more conspicuous."

"Doris, if our kids can't recognize us after all these years, something's wrong."

"Okay." The driver held onto Jamie's arm. "Tell me when you see them."

"There. Over there. I see them. Can I get Lynne now?"

"Your sister stays in the car with my friend. You walk over to them, get the phone. Don't waste time. Forget the hugs and kisses. Just get back here. We wait in the car while your sister checks to make sure it's her phone with the museum photos. Then you two can run over to your parents. Understand."

"I get it," exclaimed Jamie, crossing the parking lot to the fairgrounds until he reached the booth. Before his parents could hug him or say anything, he grabbed Lynne's phone. "I'll be right back. Don't move."

He ran back to the car, shoved the phone into his sister's hand. "Check it. Make sure the museum photos are on it."

Lynne scrolled down to the end, saw the photos and nodded. Jamie snatched it and slapped it into the driver's hand.

"Here, tell MISTER Leon to have fun with it wherever he's going!"

He opened the car door and pulled out his sister "Let's go, Lynne. They're waiting for us."

"And you two," he added. "Get an honest job. Kidnapping kids doesn't count!"

As soon as the two kids were out of the car, the driver was out of the lot and onto the roadway. He drove about two and a half miles and then stopped on a side street.

"What're we stopping for?" asked the other guy.

"The phones. Remember Leon said to destroy them. I didn't want to take time to do it in the parking lot."

He took the two phones, popped the trunk, and pulled out two heavy hammers.

"Here, have some fun." He gave one to his friend and

tossed the two phones onto the sidewalk. In a second, the two phones were smashed into pieces.

"There, that's the last of this job," said the driver.

Getting back into the car, he faced his friend and said, "Pick a direction. It's time for a little vacation."

Chapter Nineteen
Now What?

Jamie and Lynne tore across the parking field, waving their arms furiously so their parents would see them. Their legs still in race mode, they came to a dead stop right into their open arms.

Prying themselves from their parents' hugs, the twins took a moment to realize all the activity at the fair.

"We should've come here instead of the museums," said Jamie. "We would've had a great time and this whole mess wouldn't have happened."

"Right," Lynne smiled at her brother. "And we'd be on the cruise ship as planned."

Before he could return the sarcasm, she pointed to the food booth.

"Can we get something to eat? I'm starved. All they gave us all day was a small snack."

"Wait til' we tell you where we were. What a place!"
exclaimed Jamie. "There was ... "

"Not now, kids," Mr. Burton broke in. "Wait until we
get to the police station. You'll have to tell them
everything, every little detail. Just get your food for now."

Carrying their burgers and shakes, the twins followed
their parents to the fairgrounds gate where a car was
parked, a uniformed officer standing in front.

"I'm Officer Peeters. "It's a pleasure to welcome you
back." Noticing the food the twins were holding, he said,
"Climb into the back and enjoy your lunch. We'll have
plenty of time to catch up."

Mr. and Mrs. Burton kept glancing back to keep
reminding themselves that their children were really here,
really safe, eating hamburgers and drinking shakes as if
nothing had happened.

"Perfect timing," said Officer Peeters, pulling up to the
police station just as the twins swallowed their last bites. He

noticed Jamie staring at the sign above the door:

Brussels Capital Ixelles Police Zone

"That's the official term for the police here in Brussels," the officer explained.

He led them into a small room with a table and chairs. "It's been a very long day for all of us. Let's sit and relax for a few minutes."

The door opened and another officer walked in, holding a tray of glasses and a pitcher of what looked like lemonade.

"I'm Officer Janssen. We've been keeping your parents company while you two were … 'detained' … shall we say … but you're back now and I'm sure there's plenty you want to tell us."

Jamie and Lynne took turns describing the man who calls himself Leon, his mansion, his art collection.

"We saw that Fall of Icarus painting he stole from the museum, "said Lynne. "When Alfred showed us all his stuff, I couldn't believe he was gonna leave so much behind."

"Whoa!" interrupted Janssen. "Who's Alfred?"

"Alfrred is Leon's assistant," explained Jamie. "He's the fake guard from the museum, the one in the photos Lynne snapped. He sorta babysat us while Leon planned his getaway."

"Yeah," said Lynne. "I pretended to be impressed by how Leon depended on him. I found out a lot of stuff he probably shouldn't have said."

"For instance?" asked Officer Peeters.

"Leon's family is very rich and they have homes all over Europe," Lynne continued. "He's a pilot and owns a bunch of airplanes. He even has private airfields where he can land his planes."

"And - a big AND," added Jamie. "Alfred kept mentioning Madrid. He bragged that they have a home in Madrid even bigger that the one here. He said Leon hasn't been there in a while and that he has a private airfield there."

"And the famous Prado Museum happens to be in Madrid," nodded Officer Janssen.

"Time to do some research: any recent thefts in Madrid and a list of private airfields."

"But Europe is huge. Even if he goes to Madrid, what good does that do?" asked Mr. Burton. "There are hundreds of private homes there. And you don't even know his last name."

"True enough," said Officer Peeters, "But, with your kids' help, we plan on finding his mansion somewhere outside of Brussels. There must be something he left behind to give us more information. In the meantime, we can alert the Prado Museum to be on the lookout for any new museum hires and send them the photo of that guard.

"And, Mr. and Mrs. Burton, we'd like you and your children to go back to the hotel. Your bags are still there and they'll have a new room for you."

"Jamie, and Lynne, we need you to think hard. After the two goons grabbed you, about how long do you think you were in the car before you reached the mansion?"

The twins shrugged their shoulders. No idea.

"That's okay," said Officer Peeters. "Go back and relax. Tonight, we want you to make a list of anything you remember while you were in that car, anything the drivers said, any stops you made, anything unusual you saw along the way. Get a good night's sleep. Tomorrow morning we'll pick you all up at ten. We're going to find that mansion!"

Chapter Twenty
Looking For Clues

Each of the four Burtons had a restless night's sleep.

Mr. and Mrs. Burton tried piecing together what had happened these past few days. And, more importantly, **why** it had happened. Like most parents, they questioned whether it was their fault that they got caught up in this nightmare. Especially Mrs. Burton. Her thoughts hounded her.

If I'd never wanted to see that painting, we'd never have gone to that museum in the first place. And, if I wasn't so darn friendly with that guard, he'd never have known where we were staying.

Mr. Burton struggled with his own thoughts.

I should have paid more attention to Lynne when she said someone tried to grab her phone at the chocolate shop. I figured it just the hustle of the crowds in a busy city.

If my mind wasn't on meeting the schedule of the cruise ship, I might have realized that meeting that guard at the music museum was no coincidence.

Jamie and Lynne were tired. It had been a long and confusing day. As they drifted off to sleep, Jamie had flashes of the scenery they had passed.

What if I can' remember what we saw? I won't be able to help the officers find Leon's mansion. Maybe Lynne will remember.

The last thing Lynne remembered before falling asleep was her fear of being left in the car at the fair when the driver sent Jamie to get the phone from her parents.

What if there was no 'swap?' When Jamie got back with the phone, what if the driver had orders to keep Jamie and me and drop us off somewhere? Who would find us?

10:00 AM - The Burtons exited the hotel lobby and looked for the familiar Brussels local police car. Instead, a large blue van was parked at the curb. Officer Peeters stepped out of the front passenger seat.

"Morning. Are you ready for a scenic drive along the Brussels countryside?" he smiled.

"Why such a big car?" asked Jamie.

"Obviously your parents will want to accompany you," he said.

"You'd better believe it!" declared Mrs. Burton. "We're not letting them out of our sight."

"We understand," continued Office Peeters. He motioned to the twins. "Climb into the middle seats with me. Mr. and Mrs. Burton, please sit in the rear seats. The van seats nine, but I want to leave space in case we find anything at the mansion to indicate who Leon is and where they might have gone. Sometimes when people leave in a hurry, even the most organized ones, they tend to leave behind something important."

Before getting into the car, Officer Peeters spoke to his driver and handed him a map of the surrounding towns.

"We'll be driving west along Route 24. I figure we should be out of the city limits in a few miles. We'll pass the signs for the Renaissance Fair, then hopefully Jamie and Lynne will recognize some landmarks. I doubt there are many mansions along the way. More likely you'll see farmlands."

Mr. and Mrs. Burton sat quietly, lost in their thoughts.

Sure enough, they passed the Fair signs, then a gas station, a fast-food place and a motel.

"Look familiar so far?" asked Officer Peeters. Jamie and Lynne nodded a yes.

"Good," he said 'cause now there should just be countryside and farmhouses. Keep your eyes open. We're relying on anything familiar to you since we don't know how long you were in the car."

There were indeed miles of countryside, farms, barns, cattle, but nothing that caught the twins' attention. And then

...

"Wait!" exclaimed Jamie. "Back up."

A few yards back, Jamie spotted a familiar barn.

"Lynne, remember that purple barn."

"Yeah, that's the one. And not far should be that white house with the polka dots on the door and the pink truck."

"Great," said Officer Peeters. "Keep looking."

"There was an orange and black tractor with the number 34 pretty close to that white house," added Jamie. "But I don't see it now."

"It's probably out on the field," suggested Officer Peeters. "Concentrate on anything else you recognize."

More miles and nothing familiar.

"What about that General Store up ahead? Did you pass that?" asked Officer Peeters.

"No," they both agreed.

"I think we went too far. We'll turn around and check out the side roads between here and those barns and houses you saw," suggested Officer Peeters.

105

"That makes sense," agreed Mr. Burton. "A big mansion-type place would be off the main highway."

The driver made a few turns in both directions off Route 24 ... nothing familiar.

The next turn took them down a road that forked at the end. A quick right turn led them to a pond. The other direction became a road that led to a long driveway.

"That's it." shouted Jamie. "Keep going. There's the black iron gate."

Officer Peeters got out and checked the gate. Locked, of course. He grabbed a tool box out of the trunk, took out a large pliers and snapped open the lock.

"Okay," he said. "We'll drive slowly around the house."

"This is definitely it," said Lynne. "See the beautiful gardens and the swimming pool. And there's the tennis court."

When they reached the back of the house, there was the

double door where Jamie and Lynne had entered.

"We found it!" the twins shouted. "It's Leon's mansion!"

Chapter Twenty-One
Back At The Mansion

As soon as the police car stopped, the twins scrambled out and headed towards the entrance.

"Whoa! Not so fast, you two," called Office Peeters. "This is a crime scene ... just like on tv. You guys have to stay outside."

Mr. and Mrs. Burton stepped out of the car. Officer Peeters explained to them.

"Sorry, but you and the children can't come in. Please take your time and walk around the property. Explore the grounds, the gardens, whatever. Officer Janssen and I need to go through each room and look for anything - any little thing that might tell us who this Leon and his assistant are, where they come from, where they're going."

"Well, can you at least share some clues with us?" asked Jamie. "If it weren't for us, you'd never have found this place."

"Of course, now let us do our job."

Armed with gloves, plastic bags, a camera, and a crowbar, the two officers proceeded to break the lock on the door, shut off the alarm, and disappear into the house.

"Well, it looks like we're on our own for a while. May as well see how the rich half live around here," said Mr. Burton.

As the Burtons shuffled along outside, the officers began their search. They methodically went from room to room, checking furniture, drawers and closets. In the closets, they looked for clothing labels, dry cleaning receipts, contents of pockets.

"Amazing the amount of expensive clothes they left behind," said Officer Peeters. "And hardly any jewelry or photographs. I'll bet there's a safe here somewhere. We'll have to get a security team to double check."

They checked behind the beds, behind cushions, under

mattresses.

In the bathrooms, they opened medicine cabinets and looked for pills and prescription bottles with doctors' names.

In the kitchen they took fingerprints from the dishes and glasses in the sink.

"Probably from the snacks the kids said they had," commented Officer Janssen. They checked calendars for names, telephone numbers, appointments; wastebaskets for mail with return addresses and business cards.

In the library they opened books for inscriptions: To___ From ____.

At the end of the long hallway, they stopped in front of a heavy wooden door with a double lock.

"This must be the Art Gallery that the kids saw," said Officer Peeters. He motioned to Janssen. "Break it open."

Upon first glance, they saw from the empty spaces in the wall that several large paintings were missing. But the remaining pieces were museum quality works of art.

"Wanna bet that the missing ones were stolen and these were legitimately bought?" remarked the officer.

"No doubt about it." agreed Officer Peeters. "Let's take them down."

The two officers carefully removed each remaining painting and checked the backs for the names of any art dealers.

Satisfied that they had combed through each room, they slowly made their way back for a second look when Officer Peeters stopped and took a few steps back as they passed one of the bedrooms.

"There's something sticking out behind that night table," he observed.

Sure enough, there was something … a small framed photo of two men and a woman, standing in front of a car.

"Bag that one too!" said Peeters.

The two officers gathered up their evidence bags, reset

the alarm, and left by the same door.

Their audience was waiting for them.

Jamie was ready! "Did you find stuff?" He eyed the plastic bags.

The officers laughed. "Oh yes, plenty of 'stuff.' "

"Let's hope it helps to find the identities of your mystery men," said Officer Peeters.

"You promised to share clues," Lynne reminded him.

"And we will once we're back at the station. But, first, we're taking you guys to lunch. Right down the road there's a cafe, a good place to see if anyone in the area knows anything about Leon and friend. People in small towns are always ready to share local news."

Chapter Twenty-Two
A Local Stop

Anyone entering the small building with the Café/Bakery sign would immediately know that it was a local. All eyes turned to the Burtons as they filed through the door. And, when the two uniformed officers followed, all eyes were fixated.

"Morning, folks," greeted Officer Peeters. "We're just passing through, here for an early lunch." He scanned the room and then led his group over to a table for six.

Menus were on the table and a large board advertised the specials of the day, including, of course, Belgian Waffles and flavored hot chocolate. The front counter held an array of fresh crisp baguettes and delicious-looking pastries: eclairs, bonbons, croissants, macaroons, fruit tarts.

"Man, I may never leave this place, "said Jamie, licking his lips.

"Take your time and order while I strike up a chat over there with the owner," said Officer Peeters. He pulled out a photo of Leon's estate and, sauntering over to the man behind the counter, he introduced himself and asked, "Do you recognize this place?"

"Sure. That's our local Mansion."

"Do you know who owns it ... or anyone who lives there?"

"Not by name, but every week or so, we get an order for baguettes, croissants, and chocolates. Well, almost every week," he corrected himself. "There are times when there are no orders for a month or two ... vacations, maybe."

"Do you deliver them?" asked Officer Peeters.

"Nope, never been there. An elderly gentleman picks them up and leaves a generous tip." Officer Peeters motioned for the twins to come to the counter. "Can you describe this gentleman for us?"

"Certainly. As I said, he was elderly, maybe in his 60's or even 70's, white-hair, very pleasant looking, polite, good manners … sort-of like a butler."

"Has he been here recently, say, a day or two ago?"

"Hmm …" the owner paused. "Let's see, today is

Monday, the day I put out the fresh chocolate bonbons. He bought the usual baguettes and a good portion of the chocolates."

"Did you happen to see what kind of car he drives?"

"Sorry, no, I was busy boxing up his order. You might ask that family over there," he said, pointing to a man and woman with a boy about Jamie's age. "They're here almost every day."

"Yea, I seen that man," said the boy. "He drives an expensive black sedan, not new but a late model. I tried to catch the license plate so I could see who makes it. It was probably a Mercedes; they're all over the city."

"Did you happen to see any of the license plate?"

"All I could see from the window were the first three letters – EAU but I couldn't see the three numbers."

"Did you notice if there were any special letters in front of the EAU, like, for instance, CD for diplomat or M for military?"

"Nope … just regular red letters on a white plate," answered the boy.

"You're a very observant young man," said officer Peeters.

"My son loves cars. Can't wait to drive one," his father laughed. "Probably not one as expensive as that one."

"Well, you've been a great help. Thanks. Enjoy your breakfast."

"Try the Belgium Waffles," said the boy. "Brussels makes the best."

Chapter Twenty-Three
Sifting Through the Clues

Back at the station house, the Burtons and the two officers began considering what they'd learned.

"Okay," said Officer Janssen. "Let's start with the description of the man who picks up the goodies for the Mansion. Turning his attention to the twins, he asked,

"Does he fit the description of Alfred, Leon's assistant?"

"Oh, no," they both answered. "Alfred is younger than that."

"And definitely not that well-mannered and polite," added Lynne.

"It has to be Edward," declared James.

"Who's Edward? "asked both officers.

"He's the 'butler' guy," answered James. "He fits the description exactly. He gave us the snacks when we got to the Mansion ... delicious chocolates that my sister managed to scarf down, despite her so-called nerves." He avoided the nasty look she shot at him. "We didn't see Edward after that."

"What about the two guys that drove you to the Mansion and later back to the Carnival?" asked Officer Janssen.

"They were tall, rough-looking guys—didn't say much except 'Sit down' and 'Shut up.' They just dropped us off at the door," replied Lynne.

"So ..." said Officer Peeters, "the only people in the house besides you two were Leon, Alfred, and Edward. Those would be the only fingerprints we lifted. Right?"

"Right," agreed the twins. "Unless there were people there before we came," said Jamie.

"Okay, so now, tell us again what Alfred said about Leon having houses all over Europe," asked Officer Janssen.

"Lynne got him to brag about what a big deal it is to work for Leon."

"Yea," said Lynne. "He boasted that Leon's family owned the Mansion and were really very wealthy. And that Leon was a pilot and owned private planes. He kept mentioning Madrid and kinda hinted that that's where they might go."

"We've already alerted the major museums in Spain, France, Italy, England and Russia. An enormous amount of famous world art is housed within these countries," said Officer Peeters.

"What about the photos from my daughter's camera?" asked Mrs. Burton. "Were you able to enlarge them for a better look?"

"Not really good, but better than nothing. We sent the copies to the museums," he added.

"Did you find some clues inside the house?" asked Mr. Burton.

"They left a few pill bottles in the bathroom with pharmacy names. And, when we checked the backs of the remaining art pieces in the gallery, we found the name of an art gallery in Amsterdam," answered Officer Janssen. "And this," he continued, holding up the small photo. "Tomorrow we're sending a team back to the house to open the safe."

"There's nothing more for you to do right now," said Officer Peeters. "We need some time to check out the pharmacy, the art gallery and the photograph, and wait for any fingerprint matches in our system. We'd like you to stay in Brussels just a few more days, in case we need the twins for any other IDs. We've arranged for you to stay in a different hotel closer to the station, if that's okay."

"Why not," sighed Mr. Burton. "The boat has already sailed."

"We'll arrange for some kind of compensation for the boat and all you've been through," said Officer Peeters. "After all, you could become national celebrities." As the family exited the police station, he motioned to Mr. Burton

and whispered, "Don't let those kids out of your sight!"

Chapter Twenty-Four

Interesting News

The family had no sooner registered and settled into their new hotel room when Mr. Burton's cell phone rang.

He looked for a caller id but all that showed on the screen was "unknown caller."

"Don't answer it!" screamed Mrs. Burton. "It could be the kidnappers."

"Calm yourself, Doris, they're hundreds of miles from here," he reassured her.

Then the hotel phone rang.

He picked it up. "This is the Reception Desk. We have a call for Mr. Burton from an Officer Peeters. Hold on while we connect you."

"This is Officer Peeters. I tried your mobile but there was no answer."

Mr. Burton hesitated. "Um, we were a little afraid to

answer it," he admitted.

"No problem. I'd like to send a car to bring your family back to the station. We've discovered a few more things about Leon and friends."

"Fine," agreed Mr. Burton.

"Detective Janssen will be waiting out front for you. No reason to alarm any hotel guests in the lobby if they see a policeman."

Sure enough, Detective Janssen greeted them outside and, within minutes, they were back at the station.

"So ... let me catch you up on things," stated Officer Peeters. "This morning, we sent a team to the Mansion. The safe was empty. The art gallery in Amsterdam closed two years ago. And the pharmacies had no record of any name for those prescriptions."

Four disappointed faces looked up at him.

"But ... Interpol came through!"

"Interpol. What's that?" asked Jamie.

"Interpol is an organization based in Paris that coordinates criminal investigations made by police forces of member countries … sort of like an international police club," Officer Peeters explained with a smile.

"And," added Detective Janssen, "since we're pretty sure that Leon has been looting art in different countries for years, we figured they might have some information for us."

"Did they?" asked Mr. Burton.

"They did. We had already sent them the photos from Lynne's camera and the fingerprints we took from the Mansion. They identified one set."

"Was it Leon?" asked Jamie.

"Sorry, I'm afraid it wasn't Leon or Alfred. It was Edward."

"Edward … that nice polite old guy," scoffed Lynne. "What kinda crime could he commit?"

Officer Peeters explained. "It seems that Edward

Hutchinson years ago was fingerprinted when he applied for a job as a groundskeeper for a wealthy private school in New York State. New York State law requires that anyone working in a school has to be fingerprinted. According to Interpol, our Edward retired from that position three years ago, did some traveling, loved Belgium, and last year rented an apartment in Brussels. He answered an ad for 'male household help' and found himself working at the Mansion."

"Wow!" grinned Jamie. "Nice work."

"Now that we have his name and address here in Brussels, I sent two of my officers to bring him to the station for questioning. He's been working for Leon for a year now so he should be able to shed some light on the mysterious art collector."

"I'd like you to wait in another room with Detective Janssen where you can id Edward and listen. He won't be able to see or hear you."

"It didn't take long before Edward appeared. He sat opposite Officer Peeters.

"That's Edward, for sure," agreed the twins.

Funny … he looks smaller," observed Lynne.

"He was probably wearing a suit and tie, like a butler. It makes you look taller," said Detective Janssen.

Edward's hand trembled as he picked up the glass of water offered to him.

"Well, let's see what Edward can tell us." The

detective switched the ON button of the listening device.

Chapter Twenty-Five

A Credible Witness

Detective Janssen waited for Edward to take a sip of water. Then …

"Thank you, Mr. Hutchinson, for agreeing to come in to answer a few questions. It won't take long. We just need to find out a few things about your employer and you seem to be the only one we've located who can help us."

Edward settled back in his chair, a bit more relaxed.

"Let me begin by asking you how long you've worked for Leon."

"About a year and a half."

"And what kind of work do you do there?"

"A little bit of everything to keep the house running smoothly, sort of like a butler/valet/manservant. I take in the mail, shop for groceries, cook meals, send out laundry."

"Speaking of mail," asked Detective Janssen, 'how is

the mail addressed?"

"Leon's mail is addressed to Mr. Leonidas Marchant," responded Edward, speaking Leon's name with a certain pride, as if the name belonged to someone important.

"And Alfred?" asked the detective.

"Oh, Alfred has a much more common name—Alfred Smith."

Detective Janssen smiled at Edward's answer.

"And do you live there, at the Mansion?"

"Oh, no. I have my own apartment here in Brussels. But they keep a room for me when Leon and Alfred leave for a while, so I can look after the house."

"They rely on you a lot. You must be a trusted part of the household, almost like one of the family," continued Detective Janssen. "Does his family live nearby?"

Edward shook his head. "The Marchants have family and property all over Europe, although none in Belgium other than Leon. They are a very wealthy French and Greek

134

family. The French contingent makes their money from the wine industry and the Greek from olive oil."

"And where does Leon fit into the family picture?" asked the detective.

"It seems that his role in the family is to maintain the Brussels estate and add to the family's extensive art collections. He does quite a bit of traveling back and forth Europe, sometimes for days, sometimes for months at a time, usually piloting his own plane."

"Did Leon tell you all this?" asked Detective Janssen.

"Leon is very private about his business and personal life. He's not very social either. It's Alfred who's the talkative one. Alfred loves to chat … and I'm a good listener."

"What about visitors?"

"The only people I've ever seen since I've been there are delivery men. Leon receives lots of catalogs for art sales and auctions. When he's away, I assume he attends auctions because, a few days after he returns, there's often a delivery."

"I see," nodded Detective Janssen, "and have you seen his art gallery?"

"Oh, yes, many times. It's magnificent … a miniature museum."

The detective paused, careful to choose his next words wisely.

"Tell me, Edward, do any of the paintings in Leon's gallery remind you of paintings you've seen at a museum … specifically, the Museum of Fine Arts here in Brussels?"

Edward's shoulders stiffened up.

"Detective, I've been a groundskeeper for over thirty years. I know plants, trees and flowers—not art!" Edward responded sharply.

"Of course, of course," the detective corrected himself. "We appreciate all the information you've given us, especially about the Marchant family. By any chance, do you know where in Europe Leon's mother and father live?"

"According to Alfred, they live in Madrid. He's been there, showed me photographs. The mansion there is beyond beautiful."

Detective Janssen opened a small desk drawer and pulled out a small photo ... the same photo they found while searching the mansion, and placed it in front of Edward.

"Do you recognize anyone?"

Edward adjusted his eyeglasses and looked closely at the three people in the photograph.

"I believe the woman in the middle is Leon's mother. Leon is on her left and the man on the right is his father. Leon looks just like him. It must have been taken before I came to work for Leon."

"Why is that?" asked the detective.

"Because, according to Alfred, Leon hasn't been to Madrid for a few years. He's actually due back for a visit."

Detective Janssen stood up, nodding for Edward to do the same. "Thank you. You 've been a great help. I have a car outside that will take you back to your apartment."

As Edward prepared to leave, he turned around to face the detective.

"I hope Leon isn't in any trouble. I'd hate to lose a good job."

As Officer Peeters turned the sound to OFF, he and the Burtons laughed out loud.

"Now there's a devoted employee," chuckled Officer Peeters. "As long as the paycheck keeps coming!"

Chapter Twenty-Six
Sharing The Facts

After Edward left, the two officers asked the Burtons to remain a bit longer before returning to their hotel.

"We know you're anxious to get back to the rest of your vacation. Sorry it's taken a wrong turn. But it's lucky for us because you're helping to solve a number of art thefts throughout Europe." said Officer Peeters.

"Yes," nodded Detective Janssen, "The Bruegel stolen from our museum is likely just one of a chain of robberies. And, with the help of the twins, we've gathered enough relevant information to locate Leon. We have Lynne's camera photos, the family photo we found, and Leon and Alfred's last names. Right now, our department is looking into the private airfields that Leon might have used, along with the Air Controllers at those airfields. All pilots have to check their flight plan to and from their destinations. If we find the airfield that Leon took off from, we can hopefully

find his point of arrival."

"As soon as we've collected that information," added

Officer Peeters, "we can send everything to Interpol."

"Interpol sounds amazing," remarked Jamie. "Do a lot

of countries belong to it?"

"Officer Peeters smiled. "You might say so. They have

194 member countries from all over the world, a staff of

hundreds of police and civilians to manage the work they

do, including police databases of fingerprints, face photos,

travel documents, and DNA. They pretty much cover

Counter Terrorism, Criminal Networks, and Cybercrime."

"Don't forget Red Alerts," added Detective Janssen.

Anticipating Jamie's next question, he explained.

"Interpol puts out Red Alert Notices for fugitives wanted

for prosecution by member police or to serve a sentence.

They have a website with names and faces of thousands of

fugitives."

Both officers were delighted with Jamie's interest.

"So ... you think you might want to work for them someday?" asked Officer Peeters.

Jamie looked at his Dad and then back to the officers. "How do you get a job there?"

"You fill out an application, like any other job. You have to be 18 years old, preferably with a BA degree, and speak English, along with any other languages, "responded Officer Peeters.

Before Jamie could ask any more questions, the Fax machine began spitting out paperwork.

"Let's hope it found what we need." Detective Janssen brought several sheets to the desk. "Here it is!"

"It seems Leon's plane is a Light Jet Gulfstream G100, big enough to transport up to eight passengers, several paintings and other baggage. He took off from Brussels Airport two days ago to Barajas Airport in Madrid--nonstop – a 3-hour, 55-minute flight. By now, he's relaxing at

Mama Marchant's house, sipping champagne and congratulating himself on another priceless art acquisition."

"Great! We've got everything Interpol needs." Officer Peeters sighed with relief. Now we can request Interpol to notify the Madrid Police. Once Madrid locates the Marchant estate, they can issue a search warrant. I'll bet Bruegel's painting is hanging in their gallery as we speak.

"And, if Leon and Alfred are both there," he continued, "even better. If prints on that painting match either or both of those two, then we've really got them!"

"It's probably not the only painting in that gallery that's been "*borrowed*," snickered Detective Janssen.

Mr. Burton took a deep breath. "I feel like I'm watching a reality crime show."

"A little more interesting than a river cruise, wouldn't you say?" Both officers winked at Jamie.

"Interpol works quickly," stated Officer Janssen. "By this time tomorrow, the Madrid police will be knocking on the Marchants' door."

"It's been a long day. You people need to get out of this stuffy office. Go have dinner in a nice restaurant, walk around downtown, buy some Belgium chocolate," said Officer Peeters as Jamie's face lit up at the word *chocolate*.

"We'll see you back here in the morning. By then, we'll be up- to- date with Madrid."

Chapter Twenty-Seven

Farewell To Brussels

"Why do we have to get up so early?" complained Lynne, rubbing her eyes and squinting at the clock on the table next to her bed. "It's only 8 o'clock. And it's not like we're going anyplace, except back and forth to the police station."

"Exactly," answered her father, already dressed. "The sooner the officers are finished with us, the quicker we get to leave Brussels."

"Amen to that!" agreed Jamie.

"Can we at least order room service breakfast?" asked Lynne, turning to her mother.

"Mmm, not a bad idea," said Mrs. Burton, tossing aside the covers. "We deserve it. Anyway, the station will probably ring us in a little while."

"Room service it is," said Mr. Burton. "Just don't go

crazy...no steak and eggs."

Mrs. Burton was right. No sooner had they dug into their breakfast than the phone rang.

"I promise this is the last time we'll get you down here," apologized Office Peeter, "I'll send the car in an hour."

One hour later, the Burtons climbed into the police car, back to the station.

Officers Peeters and Janssen led them to a table with a folder and two newspapers.

"Before you leave to finish up your vacation ..." said Officer Peeters.

"Or go home," interrupted Jamie.

"Whatever," he continued. "Officer Janssen and I have a few things for you."

"First." He held up one of the newspapers and unfolded it, revealing the headline:

STOLEN BRUEGEL PAINTING RECOVERED

Thanks to the eyewitness identification and cooperation of an American family vacationing in Brussels, "Landscape With the Fall of Icarus" has been returned to the Royal Museum of Fine Arts. The painting was found, undamaged and authenticated, in Madrid at the home of a wealthy family of art collectors. Two adult males residing in the home have been charged with the theft. Madrid authorities are authenticating other paintings at the home for possible identification of other museum pieces stolen in recent years. All names have been withheld for security purposes.

"You might want to keep this for your vacation scrapbook," said Officer Peeters.

"And … there's more," smiled Officer Janssen. He picked up the folder and emptied it onto the table, spilling out several papers.

"Because we commandeered your stress-free vacation plans, this is a form for the Cruise Company issued by the

Brussels Police Department authorizing a refund for the

cost of the Cruise."

Before Mr. Burton could utter the words "Thank you,"

Officer Janssen held up another paper. "This is an official

Thank You from the Office of the Brussels Minister-President. It's a complimentary three-day stay at any of Brussel's hotels, should you decide to return at any time.

"And this ..." he picked up another paper ... "is a three-day pass to any of the Brussels museums, compliments of the Minister of Tourism."

"And, for the younger set," Officer Peeters said, "You can show this to your friends at home." He handed Lynne and Jamie each a certificate dated, signed, and stamped by the Brussels Police Department, thanking them for their 'invaluable help in recovering a priceless painting.'

"It's like we won a lottery," exclaimed Jamie. His grin stretched from ear to ear.

"Kind of makes up for the airport?" Mrs. Burton smiled at her son.

Officer Peeters rustled the papers on the desk. "Hmm," he shook his head. "There should be one more thing. Check the folder, will you?" he asked Officer Janssen.

Sure enough, one shake and two cards popped out. Both officers smiled at the twins. "Because we were responsible for both your phones being destroyed, we thought your dad might appreciate these." Officer Janssen handed Mr. Burton the two cards—30% discount off any purchase at an Apple store. "Apple recently opened a store right here in Brussels."

"Who would believe that one short visit to a museum would involve our whole family in a once-in-a-lifetime experience?" mused Mrs. Burton.

The officers bundled up all the papers, returned them to the folder and handed it over to Mr. Burton. After all the handshakes, the Burtons left to see a car waiting outside to drive them back to the hotel, ready to pack up once again.

"So, it's back to the airport and home?" asked Jamie.

"Well," said Mr. Burton, looking first at his wife and then at the twins, "your mother and I decided we're not ready for stress-free vacations… not yet. So, we made other plans."

"Like what?" asked Lynne.

This time it was Mr. Burton whose grin stretched ear to ear. "We rented a car and we're driving to Paris ... three and a half hours and we'll be in Euro Disney!"

"Great!" shouted Lynne, as she envisioned Paris shopping and French food. "But," she turned to her mother, "How about we stay away from museums this time?"

"Agreed," answered Mrs. Burton. "But ... maybe ... one short visit to the Louvre. I've always wanted to see the Mona Lisa."

About the Painting

"LANDSCAPE WITH THE FALL OF ICARUS" was painted around 1560 by Peter Bruegel the Elder (His son Peter Bruegel was also a painter), a famous Dutch Renaissance painter. The painting that hangs in the Royal Museum of Fine Arts in Brussels, Belgium is considered a copy since it is believed that the original was lost.

Based on the Greek myth of Daedalus and Icarus, the painting appears to be a quiet country scene of people going about their business.

It is Spring. A farmer is plowing his field, a shepherd is tending his flock, a man is fishing, a boat is sailing along. BUT look at the bottom right corner. See the legs sticking out of the water. That is Icarus - drowning! As goes the Greek myth, the young man forgot his father's warning and flew too close to the sun. His wax wings melted....and down he fell.

Why does no one notice? Not the farmer, not the shepherd, not the fisherman, not the men on the boat.

Perhaps the artist is making a statement. Bruegel believed in the natural order of things in the world. In the time that the painting was made, to have a mortal man flying was unnatural, perhaps even ridiculous. And so, we see this ridiculous image of Icarus, who dared to challenge the natural order of things.

No one notices. No one cares.

\|

LANDSCAPE WITH THE FALL OF ICARUS

by William Carlos Williams

According to Brueghel
when Icarus fell
it was spring

a farmer was ploughing
his field
the whole pageantry

of the year was
awake tingling
near

the edge of the sea
concerned
with itself

sweating in the sun
that melted
the wings' wax

insignificantly
off the coast
there was

a splash quite unnoticed
this was
Icarus drowning

About the Author

JoAnn Vergona Krapp is a library media specialist in Farmingdale, Long Island, New York. She is a former elementary school teacher in Plainview, Long Island. Her articles on children's literature have

appeared in numerous periodicals, including School Library, Journal and School Media Activities Monthly. In addition to writing, Ms. Krapp is a watercolor artist. She resides in Farmingdale, where she teaches writing and painting workshops for children.

She is a member of the national Society of Children's Book Writers and Illustrators and the Islip Arts Council.

Her children's publications are:

Have a Happy and Holiday Time, collections of holiday stories

My Dinosaur Lives Circuses, humorous dinosaur poem

Missing Treasure Means Trouble, a chapter book adventure

Trouble Times Three, a chapter book adventure

Totally Trouble, a chapter book adventure

Her books and paintings can be viewed at www.jvkarts.com

About the Illustrator

Marianne Savage is a self taught artist, born and raised in Indiana, currently living on Long Island, NY. She has authored and illustrated two of her own award winning children's books as well as  illustrations for books written by other authors.

She is a member of the National Society of Children's Book Writers and Illustrators and Long Island Children's Writers & Illustrators group.

In addition to illustrating, Marianne is a designer of needle art and craft kits and her designs are sold all over the world. She is an accomplished wall muralist, sings with a local Sweet Adeline chorus and loves all things that are silly.

Her own publications are:

Bubble Trouble, a humorous bath-time adventure

Songbird's Friendship Scale, a gentle approach to bullying

You can learn more about her art and other illustration work by

visiting her website: www.mariannesavage.com.